PENNSYLVANIA

Helen Lepp Friesen

www.av2books.com

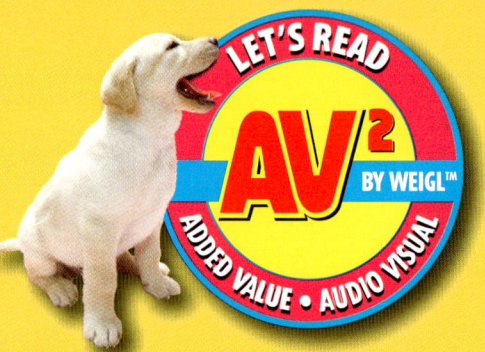

Go to **www.av2books.com**, and enter this book's unique code.

BOOK CODE

K794444

AV² by Weigl brings you media enhanced books that support active learning.

AV² provides enriched content that supplements and complements this book. Weigl's AV² books strive to create inspired learning and engage young minds in a total learning experience.

Your AV² Media Enhanced books come alive with...

 **Audio**
Listen to sections of the book read aloud.

 **Video**
Watch informative video clips.

 **Embedded Weblinks**
Gain additional information for research.

 **Try This!**
Complete activities and hands-on experiments.

 **Key Words**
Study vocabulary, and complete a matching word activity.

 **Quizzes**
Test your knowledge.

 **Slide Show**
View images and captions, and prepare a presentation.

... and much, much more!

Published by AV² by Weigl
350 5th Avenue, 59th Floor
New York, NY 10118
Website: www.av2books.com   www.weigl.com

Copyright ©2013 AV² by Weigl
All rights reserved. No part of this publication may be reproduced, stored in a retrieval system, or transmitted in any form or by any means, electronic, mechanical, photocopying, recording, or otherwise, without the prior written permission of the publisher.

Library of Congress Cataloging-in-Publication Data
Friesen, Helen Lepp, 1961-
 Pennsylvania / Helen Lepp Friesen.
   p. cm. -- (Explore the U.S.A.)
 Audience: Grades K-3.
 Includes bibliographical references and index.
 ISBN 978-1-61913-395-2 (hbk. : alk. paper)
 1. Pennsylvania--Juvenile literature. I. Title.
 F149.3.F75 2013
 974.8--dc23
                    2012015937

Printed in the United States of America in North Mankato, Minnesota
1 2 3 4 5 6 7 8 9   16 15 14 13 12

052012
WEP040512

Project Coordinator: Karen Durrie
Art Director: Terry Paulhus

Weigl acknowledges Getty Images as the primary image supplier for this title.

PENNSYLVANIA

Contents

- 2 AV² Book Code
- 4 Nickname
- 6 Location
- 8 History
- 10 Flower and Seal
- 12 Flag
- 14 Animal
- 16 Capital
- 18 Goods
- 20 Fun Things to Do
- 22 Facts
- 24 Key Words

**This is Pennsylvania.
It is called the Keystone State.
Pennsylvania played a key role in forming the United States.**

This is the shape of Pennsylvania. It is in the east part of the United States.

Where is Pennsylvania?

Pennsylvania borders six states and Canada.

7

Abraham Lincoln gave a famous speech in Pennsylvania in 1863. It was called the Gettysburg Address.

The Declaration of Independence was signed in Pennsylvania on July 4, 1776.

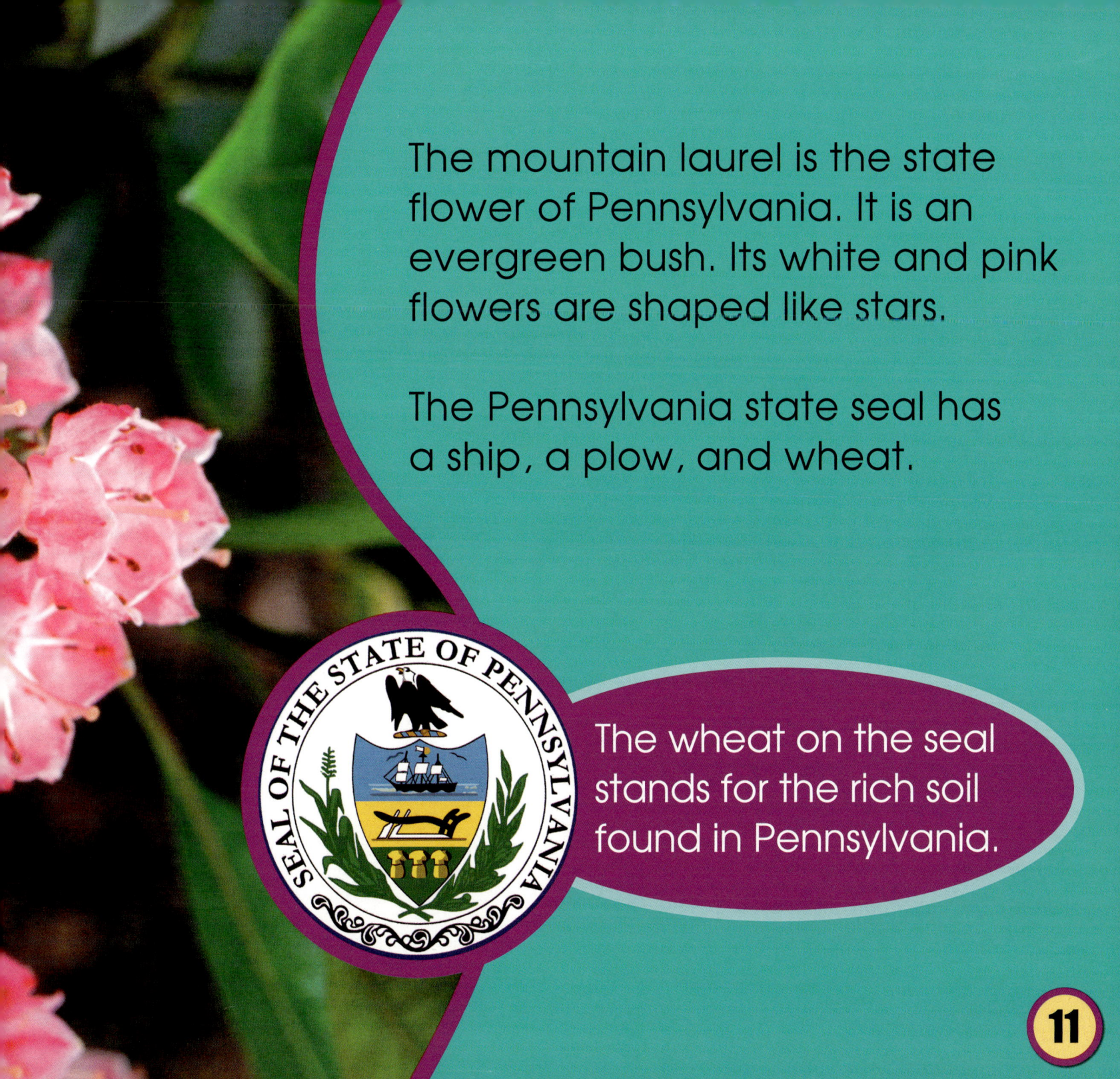

The mountain laurel is the state flower of Pennsylvania. It is an evergreen bush. Its white and pink flowers are shaped like stars.

The Pennsylvania state seal has a ship, a plow, and wheat.

The wheat on the seal stands for the rich soil found in Pennsylvania.

This is the state flag of Pennsylvania. It has a shield with an American bald eagle on top. It also has a horse on each side of the shield.

The state motto is on the bottom of the flag.

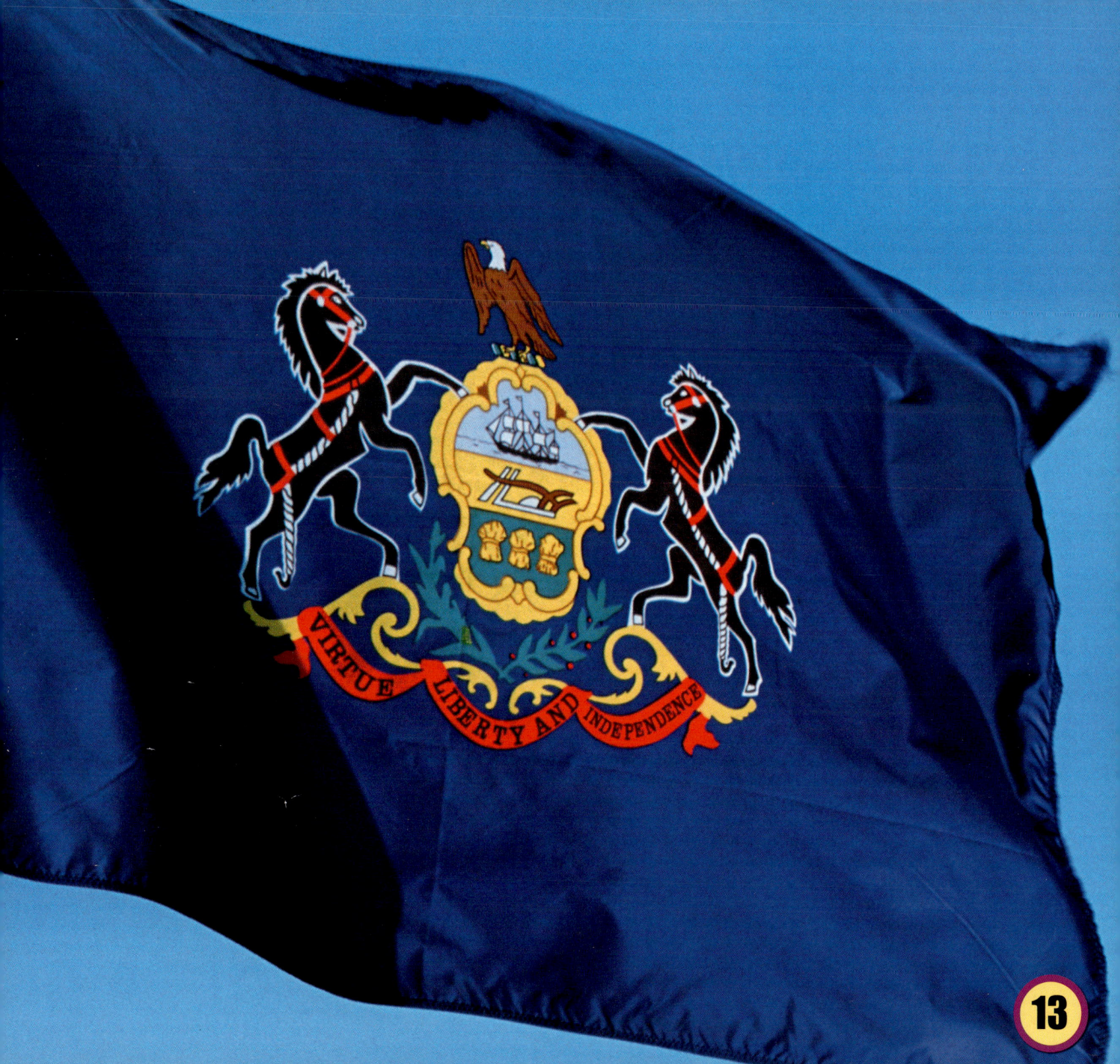

The Pennsylvania state animal is the white-tailed deer. Very few deer lived in Pennsylvania at one time. There are more than one million white-tailed deer in the state today.

White-tailed deer can run up to 36 miles an hour.

This is the capital city of Pennsylvania. It is named Harrisburg.

More than 100,000 people visit the Harrisburg capitol building each year.

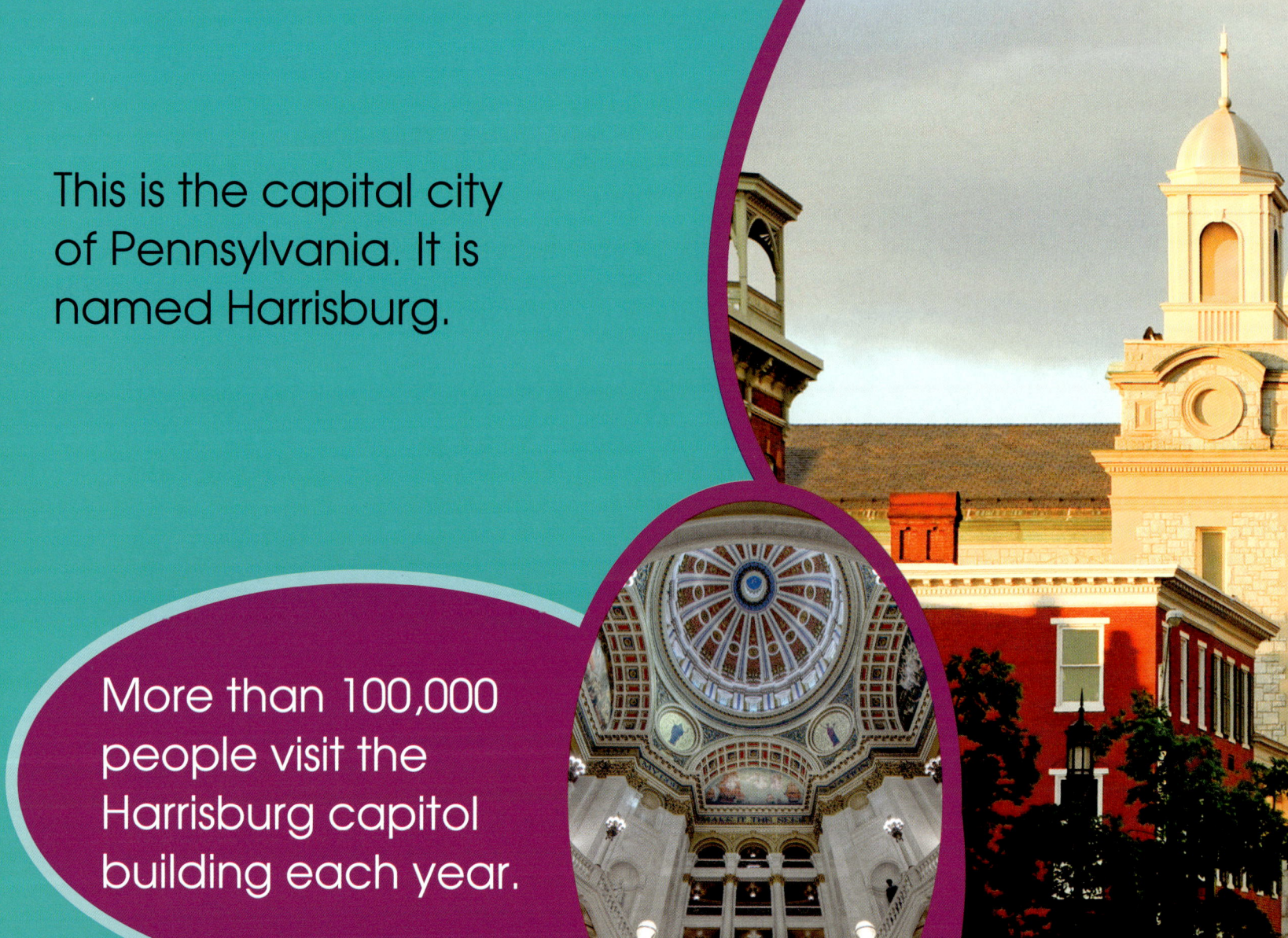

16

Hershey's chocolate is made in Pennsylvania. The first Hershey chocolate bar was made in 1900. Hershey is the biggest chocolate maker in the country.

Streetlights in Hershey, Pennsylvania, are shaped like Hershey's Kisses.

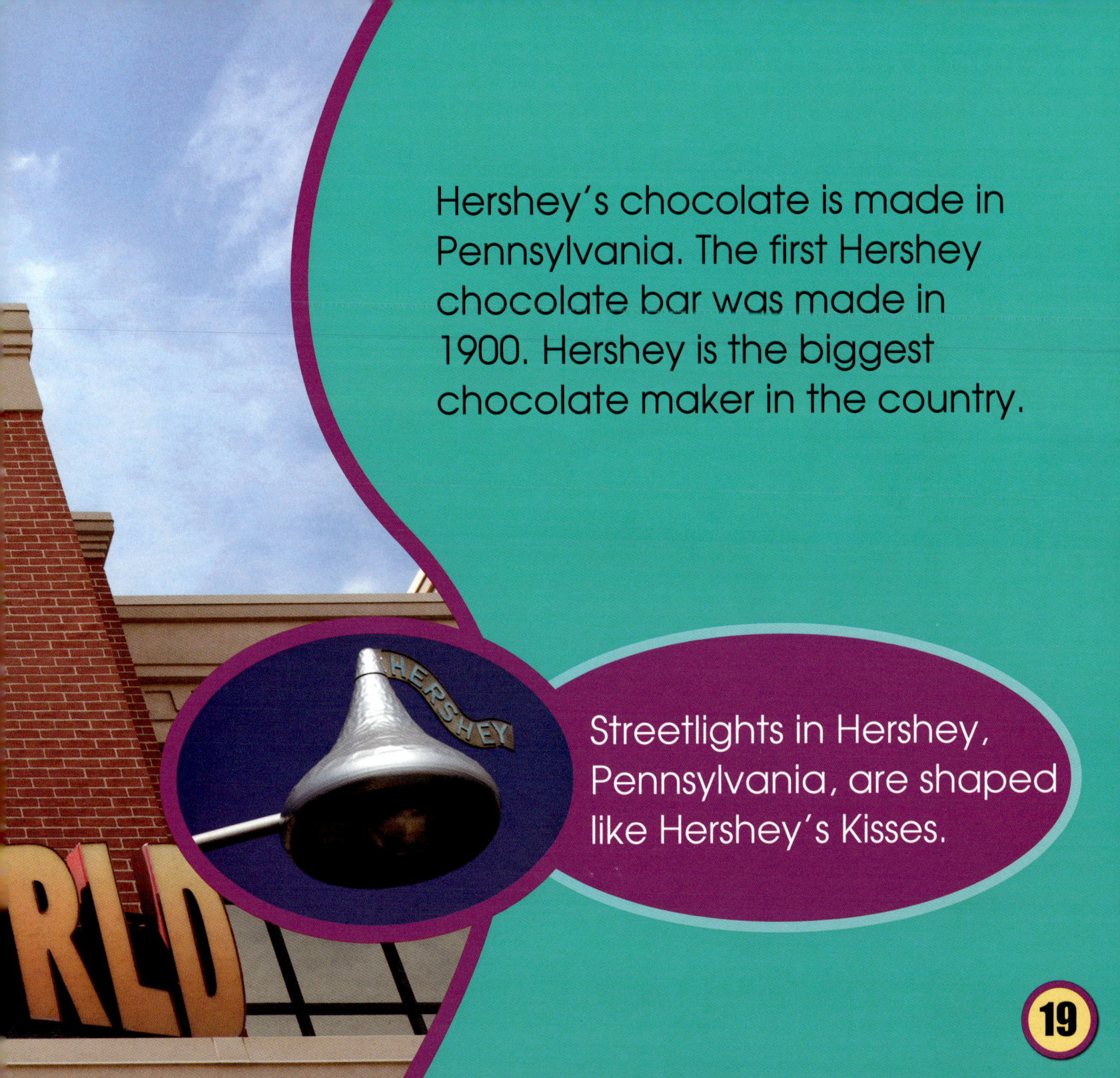

Pennsylvania is known for the important role it played in United States history. Many people visit the Liberty Bell in Philadelphia each year. The Liberty Bell stands for freedom.

PENNSYLVANIA FACTS

These pages provide detailed information that expands on the interesting facts found in the book. These pages are intended to be used by adults as a learning support to help young readers round out their knowledge of each state in the *Explore the U.S.A.* series.

Pages 4–5

Pennsylvania was named after William Penn, who founded the first colony in the area. Pennsylvania means "Penn's woods." In architecture, the most important stone in an arch is called the keystone. It holds the arch together. Pennsylvania is called the keystone state because it played an important role in the foundation of the United States.

Pages 6–7

On December 12, 1787, Pennsylvania became the second state to join the United States. Pennsylvania is located in the center of the first 13 colonies that formed the United States. New York and Canada are to the north, and New Jersey is to the east. Maryland and Delaware are to the south. West Virginia is to the southwest, and Ohio is to the west. The northwest corner of Pennsylvania also borders Lake Erie of the Great Lakes.

Pages 8–9

The American Civil War was fought from 1861 to 1865. In 1863, the Battle of Gettysburg was fought in Pennsylvania. In this battle, the northern states stopped the southern forces from invading. The battle is considered a turning point in the war. After, President Abraham Lincoln gave his best-known speech, the Gettysburg Address, at the site of the battle.

Pages 10–11

The mountain laurel became the official state flower in 1933. It is an evergreen shrub that grows in the eastern United States. American Indians made spoons out of mountain laurel wood. The sailing ship on the seal's shield represents the export of goods. The plow stands for the state's resources. The three sheaves of wheat represent the rich soil.

22

Pages 12–13 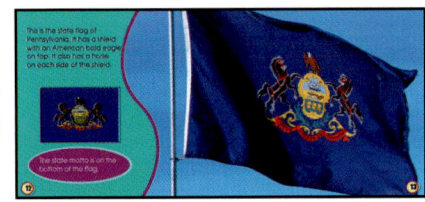 The Pennsylvania state flag is the same shade of blue used on the American flag. In the center of the flag is the Pennsylvania coat of arms. The state motto, "Virtue, Liberty, and Independence," is written on a red ribbon at the bottom of the flag. The design of the flag was made official in 1907.

Pages 14–15  The white-tailed deer became the official state animal in 1959. This deer is named for the white fur on the underside of its tail. When the deer is in danger, it runs and flashes its white tail. The deer is beautiful and powerful. It can run as fast as 36 miles (58 kilometers) per hour. It can jump over fences that are 9 feet (2.7 meters) tall.

Pages 16–17  Harrisburg became the state capital of Pennsylvania in 1812. Before this, Philadelphia and Lancaster each served as the capital. More than 49,000 people live in Harrisburg. As it is on a river, transportation is an important industry for the city. Harrisburg is home to the National Civil War Museum, the largest museum of its kind in the country.

Pages 18–19  Chocolate, cocoa, and ice cream are some of Pennsylvania's chief products. Milton Hershey was born in rural Pennsylvania in 1857. Just three years after selling his first chocolate bar, Hershey began building the first Hershey's chocolate factory in 1903. Today, Hershey's chocolate is available in more than 90 countries around the world.

Pages 20–21  Many tourists come to Pennsylvania to see the Liberty Bell, which is located in Philadelphia's Independence National Historical Park. Tourists also come to see national military parks, such as the Valley Forge and Gettysburg parks. Some people visit the "Pennsylvania Dutch" region to see the rural and simple Amish lifestyle.

KEY WORDS

Research has shown that as much as 65 percent of all written material published in English is made up of 300 words. These 300 words cannot be taught using pictures or learned by sounding them out. They must be recognized by sight. This book contains 50 common sight words to help young readers improve their reading fluency and comprehension. This book also teaches young readers several important content words, such as proper nouns. These words are paired with pictures to aid in learning and improve understanding.

Page	Sight Words First Appearance
4	a, in, is, it, state, the, this
7	and, of, part, where
8	on, was
11	an, are, for, found, has, its, like, white
12	also, American, each, side, with
15	animal, at, can, few, lived, miles, more, one, run, than, there, time, to, up, very
16	city, named, people, year
19	country, first, made
20	important, many

Page	Content Words First Appearance
4	Pennsylvania, role, United States
7	Canada, shape
8	Abraham Lincoln, Declaration of Independence, Gettysburg Address, speech
11	evergreen bush, flower, mountain laurel, plow, seal, ship, soil, stars, wheat
12	bald eagle, bottom, flag, horse, motto, shield
15	white-tailed deer
16	building, capital, capitol, Harrisburg
19	chocolate, chocolate bar, Hersey's Kisses, streetlights
20	freedom, history, Liberty Bell, Philadelphia

Check out www.av2books.com for activities, videos, audio clips, and more!

 Go to www.av2books.com.

 Enter book code. K 7 9 4 4 4 4

 Fuel your imagination online!

www.av2books.com